Black Pearl
Ponies

The BLACK PEARL PONIES series:

GHOST HORSE

JENNY OLDFIELD

Illustrated by

JOHN GREEN

Hodder
Children's
Books

A division of Hachette Children's Books

Once more with thanks to the Foster family and all my friends at Lost Valley Ranch, and this time with special thanks to Katie Foster, horse trainer and all-round equine expert.

CHAPTER ONE

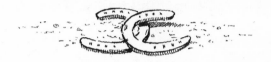

'No school today – whoo!' Keira threw back her curtains and looked out at a winter wonderland. The barn roof was covered in pure white snow and the yard lay under drifts that reached the top of the fence. This was amazing because it was the first day of May.

Keira ran to her sister's room. 'Wake up, Brooke. It's snowing!'

'Eh?' Brooke peered out from under her warm

duvet. 'What time is it?'

'Six-thirty. Get up, come and look.' Keira tugged the cover clear of the bed and dragged Brooke to the window. 'It's too deep for us to get out along the dirt road, so no school today. *Whoopee!*'

She ran from Brooke's room to the spare room where her cousin Josh was asleep in the bed opposite his buddy, Zach. 'It's snowed – we're cut off from the highway,' she said as she poked her head around the boys' door. 'Get up, let's go tobogganing!'

'Really?' Josh was the first to leap out of bed. He rushed to the window. 'Wow!' he cried. 'What happened to spring?'

'It got cancelled,' Zach said, joining him and rubbing his eyes at the sight of the snow. 'I guess

Keira's right – a toboggan is the only way to get around on a day like today.'

'Hurry up and get dressed,' Keira told the visitors. 'How cool is this!'

'Very cool,' the boys agreed, leaping out of bed as Keira ran downstairs.

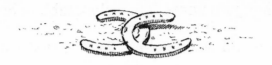

'Hey, Kevin – a storm blew in overnight.' Jacob Lucas was on the phone to his brother, Josh's dad. 'It came out of the north west, dumped about forty or fifty centimetres on us. It means Josh and his buddy are stuck here with us, but that's no problem. Actually, we can use the extra help . . . Yep, sure . . . OK, Kevin, I'll let you know as soon as we get the grader up on the track to plough our way out.'

'Hey, honey.' Keira's mom, Allyson, was already dressed and pulling on a thick pair of socks before she laced up her heavy hiking boots. 'Do you want to come with me while your dad makes more calls?'

'To feed the horses?' Keira nodded eagerly and

4

put on her own boots. Then she grabbed her thick red jacket and woollen hat. She was first out of the door, plunging into the untrodden snow. 'We can build a snowman!' she yelled over her shoulder.

Allyson grinned. 'First we feed the horses,' she reminded Keira. 'Then we have to muck out the stables, break the ice on the water buckets and clear the snow from the tack room porch.'

'We'll help!' Josh and Zach called as they burst from the house, wrapped in warm hats, scarves and jackets. They stooped to scoop up snow and make snowballs, throwing them at each other from close quarters.

Thud! Keira heard the snowballs hit their targets, turned and took one right in the chest. 'Mom!' she protested.

'Who – me?' Allyson played the innocent. But she had a twinkle in her eye and snow on her gloves.

'Yeah, you!' Keira made a snowball and threw it at her mom. It hit her on the arm.

Then Brooke appeared on the house porch and joined in. *Whizz!* A snowball flew towards Josh. He ducked and it missed him by centimetres.

Whizz-whizz-thud! Allyson was caught in the crossfire. She staggered towards the barn door then bent down, packed snow between her hands and lobbed a snowball high in the air. Whack! It fell and hit Zach smack on the head.

'Kids, puh-lease!' Jacob was the last out of the house. He pretended to groan when he saw the fight but soon grinned and joined in. He aimed and fired at Brooke then Keira – two bulls' eyes! Shrieking, the girls took cover in the barn. They closed the door after them just as a hail of snowballs landed, *thud-thud-thud!*

Neigh! From the far end of the barn, Keira's pony, Red Star, put his head over the door and gave a loud whinny. *What in the world is going on?*

'It snowed!' Keira told him, running down the aisle. She passed her mom's gelding, Captain, and her dad's mare, Misty, who both peered out of their stalls, ears pricked and listening to the fun in the corral. 'We have snow, Red Star – it means no work and all play! No school, plenty of snow fights, lots of tobogganing down the Jeep trail!'

Her strawberry roan pony nodded his head. He kicked the stall door with his front hoof. *Let me out,*

he seemed to say. *I like playing in the snow too,*
remember!

'It's still minus ten degrees,' Josh reported as he
read the thermometer hanging by the barn door.

Even so, Keira felt warm as she scooped poop
and wheeled the laden barrow down the aisle. The
stalls were almost clear and Brooke and Zach were
busy laying fresh straw while Allyson and Jacob
poured grain pellets into the wooden mangers at
the door of each stall.

Out in the corral, Keira took time out. She
pushed back her hat and rested against the rough
wooden planks of the barn door, gazing up at a
pure blue sky. In the distance, the white peaks of

the Black Pearl Mountains glistened in the sun.

'What did happen to spring?' she murmured to herself. Those little jewels of purple, pink and yellow flowers that grew in the meadow were all buried under a blanket of white. And what about the animals – black squirrels and tiny chipmunks, young deer who had only just been born? 'What will they find to eat?' she wondered.

'Beautiful, huh?' her dad murmured as he followed her out of the barn. 'But I had to call Rod Turner and cancel.'

'He's the guy who was due to bring in his two-year-old colt?' Keira realised that the snow had its downside. It meant that clients couldn't drive their young horses out to the ranch for her dad to train.

Jacob nodded. 'And Zach's pony will have to

stay in the barn until the snow melts – so no more work with that little guy either.'

Sonny, Zach's young Appaloosa, was the reason why Zach and Josh were here at the ranch. He was a pony with attitude – high-strung like most Appies. But he was doing well under Jacob's training routine, learning to trust his young rider in the round pen and almost ready to go out on the trails.

Keira sighed. 'How long before we get a thaw?' she asked, shivering as she watched Popcorn, their little ginger cat, squeeze through the barn door, take one look at the snow then quickly retreat back inside.

'Only a couple of days, I reckon.' Taking the barrow from Keira, Jacob wheeled it towards the dung heap round the back of the barn. He shrugged then grinned back at her. 'Meanwhile, enjoy!'

CHAPTER TWO

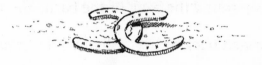

'Try this,' Keira suggested to Zach as they reached the top of the trail. It was 10.00 a.m. and Keira, Zach, Brooke and Josh had trudged through the snow up to Dolphin Rock. Below them lay a two-hundred-metre run down to the meadow.

Zach frowned uncertainly as he glanced at the black rubber inner tube which Keira was offering. The tube belonged to the spare wheel from the ranch tractor, but he pointed to the blue plastic toboggan which he'd found stashed away in the Lucases' barn. 'I guess I'll stick with this.'

So Keira hopped onto the inflated tube instead. She sat there and used her hands to paddle forward. 'Whoo!' she yelled as she set off down the slope.

Whizz-bump-whee! She picked up speed. The tube bounced and slid, skimming the surface of the snow. It was like sitting in a giant doughnut, watching the frozen world whizz by. *Bounce!* The tube hit another bump. Keira yelled and clung on as best she could. Ten metres short of the meadow fence, she launched herself sideways and bailed out into the soft snow.

'Yee-hah!' Zach yelled. He was right behind her on his toboggan, pitching off at just the right

moment and rolling against Keira, covering them both in snow.

Next came Josh on his toboggan. *Whoosh!* He hit the major bump and bailed. Then Brooke whizzed down on a second tube – bouncing, skidding and crashing right into Keira and Zach.

They lay in the snow and laughed, picked themselves up and trudged back up the hill to begin again.

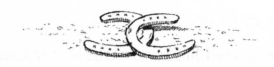

The morning wore on and they lost count of the times they made the run, switching toboggans and tubes, whooping and yelling as the snow on the worn track packed down and grew shiny.

'I swerved round the bump!' Brooke yelled, her face rosy and excited.

'I sailed clean over it!' Josh boasted, even though he'd had to hang on for dear life.

'So cool!' Brooke laughed, brushing caked snow from her jacket. She waited by the fence for Keira and Zach to follow. 'But I guess we'd better head home for lunch.'

'Yeah, lunch,' Josh agreed, turning to wave to Keira who was still up by Dolphin Rock. 'Lunchtime!' he shouted.

Brooke cupped her hands around her mouth. 'So long, see ya!' she yelled.

'Coming!' Keira called back. But she hesitated.

She was looking beyond the rock towards a cluster of tall redwood trees, their branches laden with snow. She'd seen a movement in there, wondered what it was.

'Hey, Keira, I'll take your portion of pizza if you don't get a move on!' Zach warned, setting off with the others along the Jeep trail.

'Coming!' she said again. But yes, a creature had moved amongst the trees. It was bigger than a mule deer, smaller than an elk – maybe a horse and rider, though it was too dark and deep in the shadows to really make out. 'Hey!' she called, softly at first then more loudly.

There was no reply. Whatever was hidden in there retreated out of sight.

'Maybe I'm seeing things.' Keira tutted and shook

her head. She looked down the slope to see Brooke, Josh and Zach on the Jeep trail, well on their way home. Then she took one last look towards the shadowy redwoods – was that another movement, and what had caused the snow to fall from low branches and thud softly to the ground? *No, I imagined it*, she told herself. No horse and rider would be out on the mountain in deep snow. It didn't add up. She'd made a mistake.

So, thinking of pizza, Keira jumped onto her tube and set it going down the hill towards home – *whee!*

Back home by the ranch house fire, Keira's toes and fingertips tingled as they came back to life.

'That was the most fun!' Josh grinned. He'd stuck his hat on the carved wooden bear statue which stood by the living room window and now he studied the clouds gathering over the mountains. 'And it looks like more snow's on the way.'

'What do you say we build a giant snowman in the yard?' Zach suggested. He was an outdoorsy kid from Elk Springs, the son of the local vet, with cropped fair hair and blue eyes. Sonny was the first pony he'd ever owned and he was here at Black Pearl Ranch to learn how to ride from the best teacher in the county.

As he and Josh planned how tall the snowman would be, Keira took Brooke to one side. 'I know you'll think I'm crazy . . .' she began with a worried frown.

'Yeah, so what's new?' Brooke grinned as she

picked Popcorn up from the sofa and gave him a cuddle.

'Ha-ha. But listen.' For the past hour, Keira hadn't been able to get a certain picture out of her mind. 'I think I saw a horse and rider up at Dolphin Rock.'

'No way!' Brooke insisted quickly. 'You know the temperature up there? What rider in their right mind would take a horse out in this weather?'

'Exactly,' Keira sighed. 'I told you it was crazy.'

Brooke thought for a while. 'So why didn't you check it out?'

'It was after you all left,' Keira explained. 'They were in the redwoods. It was kind of dark in there. I thought maybe I was seeing things.'

'Let's check with the others,' Brooke suggested, as she put Popcorn down and broke into the boys' snowman talk. 'Hey, Josh, Zach – did either of you happen to see a horse and rider up at Dolphin Rock?'

Zach shook his head. 'I was having way too much fun.'

Josh shrugged. 'Why do you ask?'

Keira cringed as Brooke explained. 'Keira thinks she saw them. Go on – tell them,' she urged.

'It was nothing. They were too far away to make it out properly.' She was blushing now and wishing she hadn't mentioned it to Brooke in the first place. Yeah, it was really stupid, she told herself. No one in their right mind would ride out on a day like today.

'Whoo-oo! Maybe it was a ghost!' Josh suggested, raising his arms and pretending to flit around the room. 'A ghost horse and rider up by Dolphin Rock!'

Keira blushed redder than before.

'Quit it, Josh,' Zach muttered, noticing Keira's red cheeks.

But Josh enjoyed teasing his cousin. He went on flitting and whooing and swooping close to Keira. 'It's the ghost of an old gold miner killed

when the roof of the mine collapsed way back. No, it's a cowboy who haunts the valley where he used to round up cattle. No, I know, a bank robber who was killed in a shoot-out with the cops, or . . .'

'I said quit,' Zach broke in. He caught Josh by the arm and dragged him towards the door. 'The last person outside is a wimp,' he challenged, grabbing Josh's hat from the bear statue and whizzing it high into the air.

CHAPTER THREE

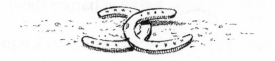

Josh, Zach, Keira and Brooke built a snowman over three metres high. They made his body big and fat then rolled a ball of snow for his head, standing on a bench to place the head on his shoulders.

'Who around here has the biggest head?' Zach asked then straightaway grabbed the striped woollen hat from Josh's head. He perched it on the snowman's head, jumped down from the bench and joined the others who were standing back to admire their work. Their man had black button eyes and a carrot for a nose. He towered over them.

'Impressive,' Jacob told the kids as he crossed the yard from the tack room to the barn. 'Now is anyone interested in grooming and feeding some horses?'

All four quickly offered their help. Keira got to work on Red Star with brushes and combs, whilst Zach tackled Sonny's knots in the next door stall. Meanwhile, Josh and Brooke wheeled grain from the store to each stall in turn.

'Take it easy,' Keira murmured to her pony as she ran the brush through his long, silvery mane and he turned to nuzzle her shoulder. 'Yeah, I know you want me to rub your nose and sweet talk you, but I have work to do.'

Red Star let out a loud sigh then stood dreamily with his eyes half closed as Keira brushed him down from head to toe.

'What do you think, Red Star?' she whispered as she worked at close quarters in the dimly lit stall. 'Was I seeing things, or was there really a horse and rider on the mountain earlier today?'

Red Star blew down his nose and shook his head.

'I know – it's a hard question. Josh reckons they were ghosts but I don't really believe in them and I don't think he really does either.'

Her pony stamped his feet then swished his tail.

'The thing is,' Keira went on, resting the brush against Red Star's neck and lowering her voice even more. 'What if there is a horse and rider up there and they're lost? I mean – it's snowed real hard and now they're saying we're getting some more snow later tonight. If you don't know the territory and there's a blizzard on the mountain, the chances are you'll soon fall into a gulley or over the edge of a cliff. Either that, or you'll freeze to death.'

'Talking to your pony, huh?' Zach's cheerful face appeared at the stall door. He had been grooming Sonny when he'd overheard Keira's voice, so he'd come to investigate.

'So?' Keira muttered. She hoped he wouldn't tease her like Josh would have done.

'Yeah, I know – I do that with Sonny,' Zach grinned. He leaned in over the door to stroke Red Star. 'I swear they understand every word we say!'

That night Keira dreamed about a ghost horse.

He was a beautiful black gelding. She saw him on a snowy mountain, standing on a high rock, silhouetted against the white background and looking down at her through a flurry of snowflakes.

'Are you lost?' Keira said to him in the dream.

The black horse reared onto his hind legs and pawed the air. Then he turned and galloped away without a sound.

She tried to follow him, scrambling up the hillside, sliding on the ice, slipping back down. She called but somehow she couldn't make her voice work – it was as if the snow was a blanket muffling every sound. She glimpsed the horse a second time – higher still on the mountain, galloping with his mane whipped back from his beautiful face, his tail streaming behind.

Then he was gone – lost in the white storm.

Keira woke with a start and sat up. Where had the ghost horse gone to? What was he scared of and why was he running away? For a while she sat in the dark and listened to silence. Then, telling herself it was only a dream, she snuggled back under the duvet and tried to sleep.

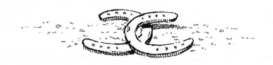

'You look tired,' Keira's mom told her next morning at breakfast. Allyson was making blueberry pancakes as a special treat. 'Didn't you sleep well?'

'Uh-huh,' Keira mumbled. After the dream about the black horse, she'd only dozed, tossing and turning until it got light. She gave Josh a weary smile as he came downstairs and sat opposite her at the kitchen table.

'There's maple syrup right there in front of you,' Allyson told her nephew as she put a hot pancake in front of him.

Josh poured the syrup then wolfed down the pancake. 'What do you say we take the toboggans back up to Dolphin Rock?' he asked Keira between mouthfuls.

'I guess,' she sighed. Today even her favourite breakfast and the prospect of more winter games didn't cheer her up.

'Are you still worried about the spooky ghost horse?' Josh was ready to start kidding around again.

But Zach and Brooke came downstairs together and Zach broke up Josh's fun. 'Maybe Keira really did see something,' he pointed out. 'I reckon we should go back up there and take a proper look – all four of us.'

'It's a deal,' Brooke jumped in quickly. Like Keira, she was upset about a possible runaway horse lost in the blizzard.

Josh agreed more slowly. 'But I need a second pancake before we leave,' he told them. 'And maybe even a third if my stomach can take it!'

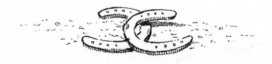

'Miaow!' Popcorn stood in the porch watching Keira, Brooke, Josh and Zach set out across the yard. He put one paw onto the top step, touched the frozen surface and quickly lifted it to flick the snowflakes clear.

'Yeah, I know, Popcorn – we're crazy!' Brooke laughed.

'Hi, Mister Snowman!' Josh said in a deep,

super-hero voice as they crossed the yard. 'Guess what we are – we're ghost-busters!'

'Hey, funny boy, I'll race you out along the Jeep trail!' Brooke challenged and they set off at a run.

Zach and Keira followed more slowly. 'Do you really think we'll see something?' Zach asked.

Keira frowned. 'I don't know. Don't tell the others, OK? But I saw the same horse last night in a dream.'

'So what did he look like?' Zach didn't make fun, as Josh would have done. Instead, he gazed at her seriously with his clear grey eyes.

'Black from head to foot – so beautiful. He was running away, like he was scared of something.'

Zach nodded and picked up his pace. 'Well,' he said, 'the sooner we get up to Dolphin Rock, the sooner we find out if there really is something to worry about.'

CHAPTER FOUR

It had started to snow again by the time they reached the rock. Large white flakes floated down from a heavy grey sky, settling on their faces and quickly melting.

'What do you say we split up?' Josh suggested. 'Brooke – you and I can take the top ridge overlooking the lake. Keira, why don't you and Zach look in the redwoods?'

The others agreed the plan. 'But stick with your

partner,' Brooke told Keira. 'Don't wander off alone.'

'And all meet back here in thirty minutes,' Zach insisted. 'If we haven't seen anything by then, we make a Plan B.'

So they set off in pairs, striding out into a white wilderness, past pointed fingers of rock capped with snow, between silvery aspen trunks, across rough ground until Josh and Brooke reached the ridge and Zach and Keira came to the cluster of redwoods.

'The problem is, this fresh snow is covering any tracks,' Zach pointed out as he crouched low to examine the ground.

'If there ever were any,' Keira muttered. Doubts had set in again as she peered between the trees.

Maybe what she had seen yesterday was a dark branch shifting under the weight of snow, or at most a poor mule deer trying to shelter from the cold.

She was losing hope, but then suddenly she did see something move. She concentrated, took a few steps into deeper shadows.

There it was again – and this time she was sure. It was definitely a black horse, moving slowly through the trees about fifty paces from where she stood. A black horse without a saddle and with no rider this time, and when the horse saw Keira he was startled. He reared and turned then galloped off, just like in her dream.

'Zach!' Keira yelled. The falling snow was melting on her eyelashes, blurring her vision. But yes – the horse was there and he was racing away through the trees, swerving in and out until he vanished.

Zach came running, too late to see. 'What?' he gasped.

'I saw him!' she cried, pointing after the vanished horse. Snow fell heavily and whirled around them, as if they were in the centre of a toy globe that had been turned upside down then shaken. 'Truly, I did! He was here – I didn't imagine it after all!'

'I believe you,' Zach said quietly. 'The question is – what do we do now?'

Keira and Zach ran back to Dolphin Rock and waited impatiently for Brooke and Josh to return to their planned meeting spot.

'We can't stay out here much longer,' Zach warned. 'The snow's too bad – we need to get back to the ranch and wait for the storm to pass.'

'But what about the runaway horse?' Glancing over her shoulder, Keira could hardly make out the redwood trees on the ridge, the snow was coming down so fast. 'We can't just leave him!'

'We have to,' Zach argued, glad when he saw two figures stumbling through the storm to join them. 'Hey, Josh, hey, Brooke – Keira saw the horse again!'

Josh seemed to be in a bad mood.

'So did you see it too?' he asked Zach suspiciously.

'No,' Zach admitted.

Josh narrowed his eyes and gave a small shake of his head.

'He was there!' Keira insisted. 'He spooked again and ran away. I lost him in the trees.' She knew now – she knew for sure that this was no ghost horse. He was real flesh and blood and he was in deep trouble.

'So let's come back when the snow stops,' Brooke suggested. She looked worried as she took off her Stetson and shook snow from its brim. 'We can bring hay, hang a net from a tree branch and wait.'

Zach nodded. 'Good plan. He'll come to eat then we can move in and put a rope around his neck.'

'That's all we can do,' Josh agreed, and the three of them set off for the Jeep trail.

For a few moments, Keira hung back. She looked up towards the redwoods, almost invisible behind thick flurries of snow.

'Keira!' Brooke called over her shoulder. 'Do you want to freeze to death?'

Keira gazed up at the grey sky and felt flakes settle on her cold face. She knew she had no choice and so she set off slowly after them.

But her heart felt as heavy as the sky as she trudged head-down through snowdrifts. She felt as if she was abandoning the poor lost horse and an image from last night's dream filled her head again. It was of the beautiful, mysterious creature rearing onto his hind legs then racing away across the snowy mountainside, mane and tail streaming in the wind – a silent black shadow against the pure white snow.

'So where's the rider?' Allyson was the first to ask the obvious question. 'Didn't you say there was a rider there yesterday?' she checked with Keira, who nodded and sighed.

'Jeez – how long before the snow stops?' Brooke wondered, staring out of the kitchen window.

'If Keira's right and she really did see this black gelding, where the heck did he come from?' Josh wondered.

Everyone was asking questions while Jacob was on the phone, calling every neighbour he could think of to ask if they were missing a horse. So far

he'd drawn a blank. 'I just called the Three Horseshoes,' he reported. 'Tom Walters says all his horses are safe in the barn.'

'So it can't belong to anyone local,' Allyson decided.

'Maybe I should call the sheriff's office.' Jacob was scratching his head. 'If there's a rider involved, we should report Keira's sighting, in case it fits any of their missing person files.'

Keira's mom nodded. 'I guess that won't do any harm.'

So while Jacob got busy again on the phone, Keira quizzed Allyson. 'How many nights can a horse survive in the snow? How long can he go without food? What will he find to drink?'

'He may be OK if he finds shelter,' her mom

explained. 'There are caves and overhangs where wild animals hibernate. And this storm can't last forever.'

'It'll be gone by midday.' Zach had been glued to the weather channel ever since they got back to the ranch. Now he interrupted with the latest update. 'Temperatures will get up to around 40 degrees Fahrenheit later today.'

'See!' Brooke seized the information and looked on the bright side. 'This snow will thaw before we know it!'

'Cool, so I can ride Red Star out to Dolphin Rock.' Straightaway Keira made plans. 'You know how good he is at tracking. I just have to show him the start of a trail and he follows it every time.'

'Whoa!' Her dad came off the phone. 'No one's riding anywhere until we're sure the storm's blown over. Besides, I just spoke with Sheriff Atwood in Sheriton – he says there's another reason for us to hold back.'

Suddenly everyone stopped what they were doing and gathered round for Jacob's explanation.

'The cops are on the trail of some big-time horse thieves. These rustlers stole horses from a ranch in Norton County then moved over your way, Zach. You're north of my brother's place at High Peak – right?'

Zach gave a worried nod. 'They didn't target us, did they?'

'No, but according to Sheriff Atwood they hit another ranch not far from you – the Silver Spur.'

'Marie Shawcross's place.' Zach was shocked. 'She breeds quarter horses. As a matter of fact, that's where we bought Sonny.'

Jacob nodded. 'Well, they stole a couple of mares and a gelding and made off with them in the middle of the night. Sounds like they're a major operation.'

'Thank heavens Sonny wasn't there.' Zach gave a sigh of relief. 'He would have been top of the list for those horse thieves.'

'Yeah, people pay plenty for a nice-looking Appaloosa like him,' Josh agreed. 'So what are you thinking, Uncle Jacob – that the runaway horse up at Dolphin Rock has something to do with this horse-stealing operation?'

'Could be,' Keira's dad said with a shrug. 'If so, there could be rustlers hot on his trail.'

As Jacob spoke, Keira felt her stomach tie itself into a knot. She went to the window and tried to convince herself that the snow was easing, that the clouds would clear and the temperature would soon rise. 'Don't worry, we're on our way,' she muttered under her breath to the mysterious black horse.

'So what do we do?' Brooke wanted to know. She turned from her dad to her mom.

Allyson frowned then gave a small cough. 'I agree with your dad,' she said at last. 'This thing with the horse rustlers could turn nasty.'

'So that's it – we hold back on the search?' Josh checked.

Keira shook her head and paced the floor.

'Until we get a call from Sheriff Atwood we don't go anywhere, we don't do anything.' It was Jacob who gave the final decision.

Keira heard the verdict and groaned. It was the worst possible news, so without saying a word, she ran out of the kitchen and onto the porch, slamming the door behind her. The snow still came down and the black horse was alone on the mountain. And right now there wasn't a thing she could do.

CHAPTER FIVE

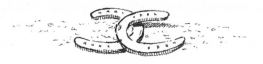

By three in the afternoon the storm had passed over, just as the weather channel had forecast. The sun came out, the temperature rose and the snow began to melt.

Keira sat in the barn, on top of a stack of hay bales, staring out beyond the dripping gutter at the disappearing snowman in the yard. His head was shrinking, his carrot-nose had already fallen out.

'In one way it's good,' she told Red Star, safe in

his stall. 'Soon there'll be grass for the horse to eat and water to drink.'

Her pony listened patiently, flicking his ears towards her and snorting every now and then.

'You know who I'm talking about?' she checked. 'I mean my black gelding, my ghost horse – only he's not. He's as real as you are, Red Star. But now they think he's escaped from some horse rustlers and they won't let anyone go up there in case the guys who stole him are there too. I guess they think it's too dangerous.'

Red Star sighed and shuffled his feet in the straw. Next to him, Sonny poked his head over the stall door as if he wanted to join the conversation.

'It's killing me sitting here doing nothing when we could be rescuing him,' Keira groaned. She

hunched forward and drew her knees up to her
chin.

'I know,' a voice said from the barn doorway, and
Zach walked down the aisle. 'It's driving me crazy
too.'

Keira slid down the stack of hay bales to join him. 'We should be up there looking. Now that the snow's melting, I'm sure I could find him before the rustlers get near him.'

'Don't even think about it!' Josh had followed Zach out to the barn and he was ready to squash any wild plan Keira and Zach might be forming. 'We're talking about a dangerous gang of horse thieves, remember.'

'But . . .' Keira sighed.

'Just don't!' Josh warned. 'You heard what your mom and dad said – we don't go anywhere, we don't do anything, OK!'

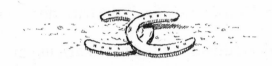

'Why is Josh acting this way?' Keira asked Brooke.

The girls had got together in Keira's bedroom after the longest afternoon Keira could remember. Now it was dark and all they could hear from outside was the constant *drip-drip* of snow melting from the roof.

'What do you mean?' Brooke asked, looking in the mirror as she brushed her wavy brown hair.

'He's taking Mom and Dad's side, keeping watch over every move I make.'

With a smile Brooke put down the brush. 'Maybe he thinks you might do something stupid like ride out and look for the ghost horse. And maybe he's right.'

Keira thought for a while about her laid-back cousin with his wide grin and twinkling eyes. 'But why?' she insisted. 'Josh has changed. Normally he'd be the one to saddle up and ride out with me.'

'Maybe because Zach is here,' Brooke said quietly as she headed for the door.

'Wait. That doesn't make sense,' Keira protested. 'What difference does Zach being here make to anything?'

'Boys don't talk about stuff,' Brooke murmured. 'So it's hard to work out, but I guess Josh is sore because he thinks Zach is stepping into his shoes. Look at it this way, Josh is our cousin, he's always been around, always been our friend, but you seem to be getting on really well with Zach and I guess it's hard for him to feel like he's being replaced.'

'Wow, so he's jealous?' A light suddenly came on inside Keira's head. 'I never would have worked that one out. Thanks for telling me, Brooke. I guess that explains a lot!'

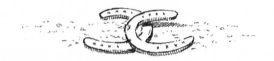

But it didn't help Keira sleep that night. *Drip-drip-drip* went the snow-melt into the gutters, and the water streamed down drainpipes until it overflowed and splashed into the yard. When Keira finally drew back the curtains on Saturday morning, she looked out on a creek that had burst its banks and turned the meadow into a shallow, shimmering lake.

'At least you get to work Sonny in the round pen today,' Jacob was telling Zach when she went down to breakfast. 'I already brought him out into the corral and saddled him up for you.'

'Thanks, Mr Lucas.' Zach was ready for action in his jacket and boots.

'And I called your dad late last night,' Jacob told Josh, who was at the table finishing his breakfast. 'I told him I'd take a look at the dirt road to see what damage the snow melt has caused. Kevin said he'd like to have you back home Monday at the latest – in time for school.'

'Yes, sir,' Josh told him. 'I'll come with you to take a look at the road.'

So Josh went off in the tractor with Jacob, leaving Brooke and Allyson to do tack room chores, while Keira offered to saddle Red Star and help Zach with Sonny in the round pen.

'Sure thing,' Zach said, looking at her with his usual bright, direct gaze.

So Keira dashed to the barn to fetch her pony. 'Hey, Red Star, how are you doing? The snow's mostly gone but now the meadow's flooded. So we get to work with Zach and Sonny in the round pen.'

Eagerly Red Star stepped out of his stall and followed Keira out of the barn without a lead rope. He sniffed the fresh air and took a quick look at the waterlogged field. Then he stood patiently as Keira put on his saddle and fastened his cinch.

In the round pen next to the corral, Zach and Sonny were already working. Zach was neck reining his young Appaloosa, getting him to change direction at walk then trot.

'Good job,' Keira called as she rode Red Star into the pen. 'Now how about getting him going at a lope and doing some flying lead changes?'

Zach nodded and concentrated on the task. He squeezed with his legs and sat deep in the saddle, sending  Sonny into a smooth lope. In spite of her worries about the gelding on the mountain, Keira began to relax.

Clockwise then anti-clockwise – Zach loped Sonny around the pen. The little Appie looked balanced and easy, and he was so pretty that Keira couldn't help but smile. 'Good job!' she called out as Tom Walters' Jeep appeared on Low Ridge trail – Reed was in the passenger seat.

'Hey, Keira!' Reed called as the Jeep stopped in

the yard. 'Did you know the telephone line is down over at Navajo Rock?'

'How come?' Keira rode out of the round pen and slid down from the saddle.

'The engineers reckon it was the weight of the melting snow – the cable snapped about thirty minutes ago.'

'How long before they can fix it?'

'A couple of hours. They were starting work on it when we left the Three Horseshoes.'

'Hey, Keira. Where's your dad?' Reed's father, Tom, got out of the Jeep and leaned one arm along the top.

'He's checking out the dirt road.'

'Your mom?'

'In the tack room with Brooke,' Keira told him.

'Good. I have a message from Sheriff Atwood,' Tom said as he strode off.

Keira pushed out her bottom lip and frowned. 'What's that about?' she asked Reed.

'Our phone line's still good,' Reed explained. 'The sheriff tried to call you but when he couldn't get through he called us instead and asked us to pass on a message.'

'Which is?' First she was puzzled, now she was tense. She felt butterflies flutter in her stomach. What was so urgent that Sheriff Atwood had to send the Walters on the three-mile trek to Black Pearl Ranch? 'Is it about the runaway horse?'

Reed nodded. 'Good news. The sheriff says they arrested those horse rustlers.'

'Cool! When? Where did they find them?'

'Last night, in a bar in Sheriton. There were two guys with a horse trailer parked outside on yellow lines. A traffic cop took a look inside the trailer and recognised two of the stolen horses from the Silver Spur.'

'How dumb is that?' Zach said as he rode out of the round pen in time to hear Reed's news.

'So cool!' Keira's heart beat fast as she thought through her next move. 'You know what this means?' she gasped.

'Yeah, the third horse from the Silver Spur is the one up on Dolphin Rock. Now we can head up there and look for your ghost horse,' Zach grinned back.

'Not "we",' Keira gabbled. 'Sonny hasn't been out on the trail yet, so he would freak out at any little thing. No – sorry, Zach, but I have to do this alone.'

Zach frowned. 'We should stick together,' he insisted.

She shook her head. 'Tell him, Reed. You can't take a half-trained pony bushwhacking up the mountain. It's too risky.'

'It's true,' Reed told Zach with an apologetic shrug.

'Red Star and I will be cool,' she insisted as she hopped back up into the saddle.

Red Star sensed Keira's excitement and skittered sideways across the yard. *Let's go!* he seemed to say.

'Tell Mom where I'm headed,' she told Zach and Reed as she set off towards the flooded meadow.

'Say Red Star will track down the runaway, no problem. We'll bring him home by lunchtime – you wait and see!'

CHAPTER SIX

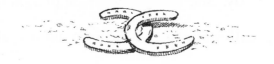

There was water everywhere. The snow had melted and gushed down the mountain in muddy streams which uprooted bushes and dislodged stones to send them tumbling and crashing down the slopes.

'Easy, Red Star,' Keira murmured as she rode through the valley. She asked him to wade knee deep through the flooded meadow, taking the shortest route onto the narrow trail leading up to Dolphin Rock.

The brave pony strode on, head held high. He was alert to dangers that Keira couldn't see, skirting round a marshy stretch by the fence then finding a safe route up the hillside.

'Good boy,' she whispered as he picked his way between half-melted snowdrifts. 'Easy, easy!'

Red Star was sure-footed but even he slipped on ice hidden under rushing water. He lost his footing and slithered back down the mountain, sliding over boulders and crashing through thorn bushes until a thicket of aspens saved them. Keira yelped, thrust out her hand and caught an overhead branch to stop their fall.

'Whooh!' She breathed out as if someone had punched her in the stomach. 'Close!' she murmured, setting off once more.

It was hard going – harder than anything they'd tried before – but they set their sights on Dolphin Rock and struggled on.

It took almost an hour but they made it, and by the time they arrived the sun was out and the air was clear. Keira reined Red Star to a halt and gazed up through the stand of redwoods where she'd last seen the ghost horse.

Red Star was breathing hard. His sides heaved in and out and a strong wind blew his mane back from his face.

'We need to find the black gelding,' Keira explained. Straight ahead lay the redwoods, to the right was the high ridge overlooking Sharman Lake where Josh and Brooke had searched. 'When we locate him we have to get close enough for me to unhitch your lead rope from the saddle horn and loop it round his neck. He doesn't know me so he may spook when I try to get near. But he'll trust you, Red Star. I'm relying on that.'

Red Star tossed his head. *Good plan!*

'I guess we start looking among the pines,' Keira

decided, squeezing her pony's sides and moving him on up the mountain. He pushed ahead, across an open area where the snow had melted, then into the shadow of the trees. The wind blew stronger, a torrent of freezing water ran between rocks, blocking their way. And so far there was no sign of the missing horse.

Another hour passed, up among the tall, dark redwoods.

'Still no sign,' Keira muttered, leaning out of the saddle and studying the ground for prints. She'd taken Red Star in and out of the trees, searching everywhere. Clouds had come in from the west. It felt cold again.

But Red Star wouldn't give in. Feeling Keira's energy sag, he took his own decision and stepped out beyond the stand of trees, on up the mountain until they came to a razor wire fence.

'OK, so this is where Black Pearl land ends,' she pointed out. 'It's National Forest land beyond the fence and we don't have a permit to go there.'

But Red Star stood firm, head up and sniffing the air.

'Anyway, there's no way through,' she pointed out, studying the fence's sharp and dangerous spikes.

Still Red Star wouldn't back off.

'Oh yeah, I see.' About ten metres to their right, Keira spotted a break in the fence where the post was down and the wire lay flat along the ground.

She hesitated. So they had no permit, but Red Star definitely wanted to step through the gap. *This way! I'm telling you – this is the direction we need to go!* 'OK,' she decided. She gave him his head and let him pick his own way through the trailing wire.

But now they were stepping onto territory which Keira didn't know. The hillside was scattered with dark clumps of trees, fingers of rock and huge boulders that she didn't recognise. Hidden gulches led nowhere; tumbling waterfalls were hard to cross. 'Oh Jeez!' she said softly. She glanced over her shoulder, thinking that maybe they should retrace their steps before they got totally lost.

But no – Red Star wanted to go forward. He took her higher, to where snow still lay in deep drifts, down a gulch that seemed to have no exit.

'Are you sure?' Keira asked him, peering into the narrow space between two steep cliffs.

Red Star stopped, pricked his ears and listened. He waited.

Keira studied the grey cliffs to either side, peering down the narrow gulch. Then she glanced at the ground and saw the signs – horseshoe-shaped prints in slushy brown snow. 'Yeah!' she murmured. It was all the proof she needed that the runaway horse had been here not long before. 'Good boy, Red Star. I knew you could do it.'

CHAPTER SEVEN

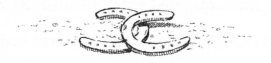

Keira saw the prints and slid down from the saddle. She crouched close to the ground to examine them. She touched them with her fingertips. Then she stood up and took another look around.

This was an odd place for the black gelding to take refuge, she told herself. The gulch was dark and gloomy. There was nothing for a horse to eat here, and there was no way out except the way that he'd entered. 'Weird,' she murmured. She walked two or three paces deeper into the gulch, far enough to see a rocky overhang at the far end, and beneath it an arched entrance into what looked like a cave. The entrance was piled with brushwood that had gathered over the years and a dead tree had fallen across it, blocking it completely.

Keira frowned then shivered. The place didn't feel good. Something about it made her want to jump back in the saddle and run. But the prints told her that her ghost horse had been here and that she had to investigate. 'You stay here,' she told Red Star, and she set off on foot down the gulch.

She'd only taken about twenty paces when she came across a slab of stone fixed upright into the ground and on it a carved inscription. Once more

she crouched down to brush it with her fingers.

Keira saw that the words were roughly carved and half hidden by moss so it took her a while to work out the name – Amos Hope – followed by a date, 1878. She rubbed away the moss then read again – 'Amos Hope –1878' and beneath it 'R.I.P.' in crude lettering worn by wind and rain. With a sharp intake of breath Keira stood up.

Who was Amos Hope? How had he died? And why bury him here? She glanced back at Red Star standing uneasily at the entrance to the gulch. Then she turned to look more closely at the cave entrance – not a cave, in fact, but a mine with a rotting door hanging from its hinges, half hidden by the fallen tree trunk. 'Guess what – we just found an old gold mine!' she called back to Red Star. 'And a miner's grave dating way back. How spooky is that!'

The wind blew down the gulley, it whistled through the trees. Shadows moved. The place seemed alive with the history of desperate men digging for gold, risking death, finding a final resting place in the rocky ground.

'Maybe what you saw wasn't real. Maybe it was

a ghost,' Josh had teased right at the start.

And now Keira imagined another ghost in the moving shadows – the tall, silent figure of Amos Hope staring down at her, his black horse loping along the ridge, mane flying in the wind.

Keira shuddered and backed away from the gravestone. She was sure someone was watching her, that she wasn't alone. She stumbled over a rock, overbalanced, fell to the stony ground. 'Ouch!' She looked down at her hand and saw that she had a small cut across her palm.

Red Star saw her fall and came towards her, head down and neck stretched.

'I'm OK!' she told him. She stood up with her legs shaking and her head spinning so much that she had to rest against the old gravestone. Who was watching her? Was it really the ghost of the old miner? Had she made up the whole thing about the ghost horse, like Josh had said?

Red Star joined her, then waited uneasily. He let Keira take his reins and lean against his shoulder to steady herself. His ears were back, his eyes rolling. *Let's get out of here!*

Shadows moved, twigs snapped in the entrance to the mine.

Keira gasped and struggled to put her foot in the stirrup. She pulled herself up into the saddle and turned towards the exit. 'Yeah, let's go,' she murmured.

Nervously Red Star set off. But then he stopped. He pranced and half turned, back towards the old mine. Twigs cracked, branches moved in the shadows. He didn't seem to know which way to go.

Trying not to panic, Keira took a deep breath. 'Let's get out of here,' she insisted.

He tried again – two, three, four steps towards the exit. Then he froze and planted his feet and braced his legs, so that Keira knew he was too scared to go on.

Her heart thudded as she whirled Red Star back round to face the entrance to the mine. She saw something – a dark shape emerging from the brushwood, clambering over the fallen trunk – not a ghost but a real live creature.

'It's a bear cub!' Keira cried out in relief. 'The old mine shaft is his den!'

The cub was tiny, only weeks old, barely able to scramble over the trunk, calling out with high, helpless grunts. A baby Black bear, soft and furry, clumsily tumbling from the trunk to the ground, rolling over and crying for his mom.

Behind Keira and Red Star, in a tall redwood tree at the entrance to the gulley, a large shape loomed. The branches shook, a deep growl filled the air as the mother bear descended.

Red Star was frozen to the spot, nostrils wide, eyes staring wildly. He and Keira were trapped between a dead end and an angry bear.

Keira sat in the saddle, feeling her heart pound against her ribs. Momma bear swung down from the tree. Branches snapped under her weight, her feet thudded as she hit the ground. Raised high on her hind legs, she faced Red Star and Keira and lumbered towards them.

CHAPTER EIGHT

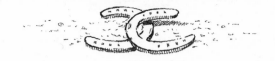

The bear was twenty paces from Keira and Red Star. Her head was back, her teeth bared in an angry snarl.

Red Star didn't move. Fear filled the air.

Keira knew that standing between a mother bear and her cub was one of the worst places to be. The momma would fight to the death if she thought her cub was in danger. And she was unbelievably huge as she lumbered towards them on her hind legs, her black shape seeming to fill the exit to the gulch. Her huge snarling head, her razor-like claws mesmerised Keira and made Red Star tremble.

Jeez, if Red Star is scared, what chance do we have? Keira thought. She could almost hear the thud of the bear's feet hitting the ground and shaking it, she could smell the sharp stench of her thick, matted fur.

Keira forced herself to think straight. Black bears don't attack unless you threaten them. The trick is not to run away but to make yourself look big and calm. 'Don't panic, Red Star,' she murmured, holding him on a tight rein. 'Let's take it easy.'

He trembled but he stood firm as the bear approached. Behind them they could still hear the piping cries of the baby and the twigs snapping as he scrambled through the brushwood.

'Hey, bear,' Keira murmured, using pressure from her leg to move Red Star cautiously to one side. She decided not to look the momma straight in the eye, knowing that animals usually read this as a challenge. So instead she stared at the ground as she eased Red Star sideways, giving the bear space to pass by. 'We're your friends, we don't mean you any harm,' she whispered. 'You go to your baby and take care of him.'

Ten paces from them, the bear hesitated, her giant front paws dangling in front of her massive chest. Her claws gleamed in a narrow ray of sunlight as she turned her gaze from Keira and Red Star to the cub then back again.

'Go ahead,' Keira encouraged.

Momma bear dropped onto all fours and loudly sniffed the air. She took a few more steps into the gulch until she was level with the intruders.

Red Star trembled but Keira sat quite still. She kept on the pressure with her leg, praying that her pony didn't rear up and strike out at what must seem like the biggest threat.

Momma stared at them. She sniffed again. She turned her head towards her baby who had made it through the brushwood and was running towards her. Would she pass on by and meet her baby?

Keira held her breath. *Look down at the ground, don't challenge, sit quiet and count the seconds. Four, five, six . . .*

A low growl rumbled from deep in the bear's chest up into her throat. She took a final sniff at the ground where Red Star stood then decided to move on. Baby scampered towards her, Momma padded forward, Baby threw himself at her and clung to her as together they headed back towards the mine.

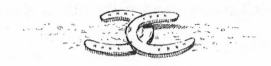

'You're such a star!' Keird told her pony as slowly, without any fuss, she eased him out of the gulch. The danger was over. They were free to carry on with their search.

She breathed again, only pushing Red Star on into a trot once they were well clear of the bear and her cub and heading across National Forest land towards the next ridge.

Now she could look out for more telltale signs –

mainly hoofprints but also piles of recent droppings and even stray hairs from the runaway gelding's mane or tail that had got entangled in a bush or a low branch. She was searching so hard that she failed to pick up the sound of hooves galloping up the mountain towards them.

Red Star heard. He reached the ridge, stopped and looked back.

'What is it?' Keira asked. She glanced over her shoulder to see a pony and rider approaching fast. 'That's Annie,' she muttered, straight away recognising her sister's sorrel mare. 'And Josh!' she said, her voice rising in surprise.

'Hey, Keira!' Josh called. He and Annie soon joined Keira and Red Star. His hair was whipped back by the wind and his pony was breathing hard.

'I'm glad you spotted us – Annie needs to take a break.'

'Hi, but what are you doing here?' she wanted to know, remembering the hostile way Josh had been acting recently.

'I guessed you could use some help finding your ghost horse,' he grinned. 'Zach told us you turned down his offer, so I asked Brooke if I could borrow Annie and we managed to track you down.'

'Yeah, Sonny would've spooked out here on the mountain,' she explained, still cautious.

'So are you pleased to see me?' Josh wanted to know. He patted Annie's neck and waited for her to stop sucking in air and for her sides to stop heaving.

'Only if you're serious about helping me,' she warned. 'I don't want any whooo-whooo jokes about me seeing horses that don't really exist.'

There was a pause. The smile slipped from Josh's face and he grew serious. 'I'm sorry I gave you a hard time, Keira. I was out of order.'

Her eyes widened. 'You mean it?'

Josh nodded and blushed. 'Really – I'm sorry for

the way I've been acting, so I came to lend a hand. Is that OK?'

'Thanks.' Keira was relieved they were now reading from the same page. And she had to admit that deep down she was glad to see Josh. She told him about the bear and her cub. 'It was pretty scary,' she admitted.

'And still no sign of the runaway horse?' Josh checked.

'I've been following tracks and Red Star knows what he's doing, for sure. He's the one who wanted to cross over on to National Forest land. And you know me – I trust my pony one hundred per cent!'

'Your dad followed me in the Jeep with Brooke and Zach.' While Annie rested, Josh filled Keira in on events. 'They have to stick to the trails but they gave me this so we could keep in touch.' Reaching into his saddle bag, he drew out a chunky two-way radio with a small antenna – a device which Jacob sometimes used to check in with the ranch when he took young horses out on the trail. He switched it on and spoke into it. 'Zach, Josh here. Do you read me? Over.'

Keira listened to Zach's crackly response. 'I hear you, Josh. Over.'

'I located Keira and Red Star. Over.'

'Cool. Are they OK? Over.'

'Yeah, they're both good. We came through a gap in the fence and we're on National Forest territory. Over.'

'Can you give us a landmark? Over.'

Josh turned to Keira. 'Have you any idea where we are?'

'Half a mile north of the old gold mine,' she told him, believing that her dad would recognise the description. 'The one with Amos Hope's gravestone.'

Josh spoke again into the radio. 'North of where Amos Hope is buried,' he reported. 'Over.'

'Gotcha,' Zach replied. 'We're heading that way with the trailer right now. Over and out.'

Josh switched off the radio and put it back in his saddle bag. 'That's our back-up team in place,' he grinned at Keira. 'Now all we have to do is find our ghost horse.'

CHAPTER NINE

They rode on across the thawing mountainside. Water gushed down rock faces and cascaded over waterfalls. The ponies splashed through creeks and sank knee-deep in boggy ground.

Red Star led the way, stopping every so often to raise his head and listen intently.

'What can he hear?' Josh asked.

Keira strained her eyes and ears. 'I don't know,

but he's definitely picking up something,' she said quietly, giving Red Star his head again and trusting him as always. They were still heading north, way off the beaten track.

It was when they rode clear of a clump of pine trees and began to step across a flat stretch of bare granite that Keira picked up another sign of her elusive ghost horse. There, caught on a low thorn bush growing out of a crack in the rock, was a wisp of black tail hair. She slid quickly from the saddle and pulled it free, held it up between her fingers to show Josh.

'He really did come this way,' Josh agreed.

Keira took a deep breath. 'Good job, Red Star.' She felt her hopes rise as she stepped back into the saddle and they rode on. 'And look!' she said when they cleared the rock and found themselves on wet sandy ground. She pointed to hoofprints, followed them on up the mountain and into another stand of pines.

They rode between the trees into deep shadow, waiting for their eyes to get used to the darkness. Red Star and Annie trotted side by side, straining forward, letting their riders know that the search was almost over.

'He has to be around here somewhere!' Keira breathed.

'I guess he knows we're here,' Josh agreed. 'He probably heard us following him and took cover.'

'Red Star, please tell him we only want to help.' Talking in a whisper, edging forward between the rough-barked trees, the search went on until they came to a rocky ledge and a sudden drop into a gulley where a fast-running creek splashed over rocks.

'He must have turned back,' Keira murmured as Red Star teetered at the edge. 'Which way did he head – up or down the hill?'

'Let's try downhill,' Josh suggested, turning Annie and letting her pick her way between boulders.

Keira and Red Star followed.

'I see a print in the mud here!' Josh called over his shoulder. He let Annie take him down to the next platform of rock, close to a tumbling waterfall, then he waited for Keira.

She joined him on the small ledge where spray from the waterfall rose and chilled their faces. 'He's sure not making this easy,' she sighed, peering down the hill and suddenly spying a faint shape through the mist. 'There!' She pointed.

Josh wiped his wet face with the back of his hand then followed her pointing finger.

'Do you see him?' she hissed. It was their runaway gelding, standing at the bottom of the waterfall, sheltering between two aspen trees. He was looking up at them, ready to take flight if they came nearer.

'Yeah, I see him.' Josh looked uncertain. 'What do we do now?'

'There's only one way down,' Keira decided. 'I'll lead, you follow.'

They kept close to the side of the tumbling creek, leaning far back in the saddle and swaying from side to side as they went down. Below them, the runaway horse watched anxiously.

'Good boy, Red Star – we're almost there.' Keira could see the gelding clearly now. He looked bad – his black mane was tangled, his head collar was frayed and his ribs poked through his skinny sides. And he was scared. He trembled and laid his ears flat against his head.

'Take it easy,' Josh warned from behind. He felt Annie miss her footing and slide on the wet rock.

At last Red Star and Keira reached flat ground. They were maybe ten paces from the gelding. 'Hey, boy,' she breathed, leaning forward to unhitch the coiled rope from her saddle horn.

The gelding backed away, right up against a tall rock.

'It's OK. We're going to take you home to Black Pearl Ranch. We'll feed you and take care of you – you can trust us.' She'd unhooked the rope and begun to form a lasso when it all went wrong.

A man suddenly appeared on top of the rock behind the ghost horse. He was wearing a dripping Stetson and a thick chequered jacket, his shadowed face was unshaven, thin and mean.

The gelding sensed him but couldn't see him. Josh yelled out a warning to Keira as the guy began to scramble down the rock.

'Stay back!' the stranger yelled at Keira as he slid down. 'Don't lay a finger on my horse, you hear!'

Keira held Red Star on a tight rein. 'He's a runaway,' she argued. 'Stolen by rustlers, but he escaped.'

'Back off,' the guy repeated as he lunged to grab hold of the gelding's head collar. 'I tell you, this is my horse!'

The gelding reared up. He struck out at the man with his front hooves.

Red Star gave a shrill whinny. Annie spooked. She turned on her rocky ledge, lost her footing, slipped sideways towards the waterfall. Very afraid, she sat back on her haunches and slid with Josh into the back of Red Star. The legs of both horses buckled and they went down on their sides while their riders threw themselves clear in the nick of time.

Josh was first on his feet, reaching into his saddle bag for the two-way radio to call for help. The stranger saw the radio in his hand and gave an angry yell. He came at Josh, grabbed the radio and flung it against a rock. It lay in pieces by the waterfall. Then the man turned on Josh and shoved him against the jagged rock. Josh hit his head, slumped to the ground and lay still.

Terrified, Keira cried out. Annie and Red Star struggled to their feet while the gelding reared again. Before Keira knew it, the stranger had grabbed the rope from her hand. 'This is just what I don't need – a couple of kids playing sheriff and getting in my way,' he snarled. Quickly and expertly he whirled the lasso and threw it. The noose landed around the gelding's neck. He pulled it tight.

'Stop!' Keira cried. She tried to wrestle the rope back, but the gelding's hooves crashed down, brushing her face and shoulder, forcing her back.

Again, before she could react, the guy reached out and grabbed Red Star's reins. Still holding the end of the lasso, he stepped into the saddle. 'I'm warning you – don't follow us,' he told Keira.

She gasped as she watched him rein Red Star towards the creek, tugging the gelding after him. Red Star plunged in and the water crashed against him. He held steady, waded across the creek and made it to the far bank, dragging the ghost horse with him.

'Come back!' Keira cried. 'Red Star, don't go!'

But the stranger spurred him on, kicking him hard across a rocky slope into a thicket of willows.

Keira felt every cut of the spurs against her beloved pony's sides. She gasped again and fell to her knees beside Josh. 'Wake up!' she begged. 'He's got the ghost horse. He's taking Red Star!'

Josh lay with his eyes closed, one arm flung to the side, his fingertips touching the broken radio.

Keira glanced up in time to see the thief disappear into the willows with Red Star and the ghost horse. She looked down again at Josh and knew that she couldn't leave him. 'Josh, wake up,' she sobbed. 'Can you hear me? Please wake up and help me decide what to do!'

CHAPTER TEN

I t seemed to Keira that an age went by before Josh's eyelids flickered open. The horse thief was already out of sight and all that could be heard was the crash and splash of the waterfall close to where Josh lay.

'What happened? Where am I?' he stammered as he woke up.

'You hit your head. The guy got away on Red Star.' The words were out of her mouth and now the situation was more real, more shocking than ever. Keira shuddered as she helped Josh to raise himself onto his elbows. 'Can you do this?'

He nodded but found that the movement hurt his head. 'Ouch! He busted the radio as well as my head, right?'

'Yeah, we can't contact the others. This is scary, Josh. What are we going to do?'

'You take Annie and follow him. I'll be fine.'

'I can't do that,' Keira sighed. She looked longingly in the direction the thief had taken but she knew Josh needed her. 'I have to get you back to the ranch. Come on, I'll ease you into the saddle.'

Very slowly Josh got to his feet, but his legs were shaky and he had to hang onto Annie's saddle horn to stay upright.

'Dizzy?' Keira checked.

He nodded. 'Ouch, my head! I forgot. Hey, am I hearing right? Is that a car engine?'

Keira listened hard. From the direction the thief had taken there was definitely the faint sound of a motor starting up. 'On the far side of those willows – there must be a road.'

Josh groaned. 'The guy's making his getaway. You have to stop him.'

The engine roared above the sound of the waterfall – it was a big vehicle, coughing and spluttering into life. Keira pictured the thief loading the ghost horse and Red Star into his trailer, getting ready to drive away.

'Go ahead, Keira – go take a look!' Josh urged, still leaning heavily against Annie.

So she left Josh and ran across the boggy ground, through the willows, her heart pounding, until she reached a clearing and saw what they'd both feared – the sight of an old white trailer with a dented fender and a missing registration plate. It was parked on a dirt road, the rear doors securely bolted and the guy in the Stetson at the wheel.

'Stop!' Keira's voice was hoarse, her throat dry. She sprinted towards the trailer, saw the driver release the brake and edge forward.

The heads of two horses appeared at the rear door – one black, one silvery-grey; the gelding and Red Star. They saw Keira and began to call – high, shrill whinnies that signalled danger.

She ran towards them even though she knew it

was risky to show herself. The driver looked in his mirror, saw her and put his foot on the gas. His wheels threw up a spray of sharp grit that pelted Keira's legs and arms. She put up her hands to shield her face. 'Please, don't take Red Star!'

If the thief heard her, he didn't pay any attention. Down went his foot. The old engine roared and he sped off down the track.

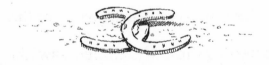

What seemed like another age went by as Keira sprinted back to Josh and told him what she'd seen. 'A white trailer . . . old, beaten up . . . the ghost horse and Red Star in the back.'

Slumped against Annie's saddle, Josh groaned. 'We need to tell someone.'

'Can you ride?'

'I can try.'

Keira helped him up then slowly she began to lead Annie back the way they'd come, all the time wondering where the guy was heading and what would happen to Red Star when he reached his destination.

'Try not to think about it,' was Josh's advice.

'Yeah, Red Star can take care of himself,' she sighed.

'He's smart. He'll find a way to escape.'

Keira wanted to believe it, but the doubts came rushing in. 'The guy looked mean.'

'I guess he's mad that the cops caught the other members of the gang.' Josh's voice was slow and slurred, his head swam.

'What if he takes it out on Red Star?' The idea brought Keira to a halt on the ridge overlooking the waterfall. 'I can't bear to think about it!'

She turned to look up at Josh but there was no answer. His head hung forward, he swayed in the saddle. He was about to faint, she realised.

Just then Annie raised her head and whinnied. The call carried down the mountain, through the pine trees and on towards Black Pearl territory. She called once, twice, three times.

Then three figures appeared on foot, out of the shadow of the trees, running towards them. Jacob led the way, ahead of Brooke and Zach. He spotted Josh slumped forward in the saddle and Keira leading Annie along the ridge.

'Dad?' At first Keira didn't believe her eyes, but

Annie kept on whinnying and they kept on sprinting.

'Hang on in there!' Jacob yelled. He ran the final stretch, just in time to catch Josh as he finally lost his balance and fell sideways from Annie's back. Quickly they carried Josh to the Jeep and laid him on the seat.

'Brooke, you ride Annie back home. We'll drive straight to the hospital,' Jacob decided. 'Josh needs an X-ray.'

Zach and Keira piled in beside Josh and sat in silence as Jacob raced towards the hospital. He took Low Ridge Trail, out past the Three Horseshoes and onto the highway south of there. Each bump, each swerve brought a low groan from Josh as he lay, eyes closed.

'Don't worry, we'll soon be there,' Zach promised.

They sped along and soon Keira and Zach gazed out at the houses on the outskirts of Elk Springs. They passed the football stadium and the equine medical facility, stopped for red lights, started again and finally reached the hospital in the centre of town.

'Zach, run inside for help,' Jacob ordered as he screeched to a halt by the main door. 'Keira, keep talking to Josh. Try and wake him up.'

'We're here at the hospital,' Keira told her cousin. 'The doctor will check you out – you'll get an X-ray, everything will be cool.'

Lying motionless on the back seat, Josh's eyelids fluttered but didn't open.

'Wake up,' Keira pleaded. She pulled gently at his sleeve.

Slowly Josh opened his eyes. When he spoke, he sounded dazed and confused. 'Hey, Keira – did you catch the horse thief?' he mumbled.

'Not yet, but we will. First we get you into the hospital.'

'I'm cool,' he protested feebly as Keira stepped back to allow the medics to take charge.

They came and lifted Josh out of the car onto a gurney then they pushed him towards the sliding doors. Inside the ER there were nurses to check him over and hook him up to machines, a woman behind a desk asking Jacob for information about the patient – name, age, address, closest family member. To Keira it was all a blur of lights, screens, corridors and doorways, of people in uniforms running here and there.

Zach stood beside her and saw that she was shaking. He grasped her hand. 'Josh will be fine,' he insisted. But his own lip trembled and he fought back the tears.

'The guy shoved Josh and Josh bashed his head

against a rock. I couldn't call you because he smashed our radio too,' Keira sobbed.

'I hear you,' Zach soothed. 'It's going to be OK.'

Keira shook her head and let the tears fall. 'No, it's not. He put a rope around the ghost horse, he took Red Star . . .'

'We'll find him,' Zach said gently.

Lifting her head, Keira looked her in the eye. 'What if we don't?' she whispered, her voice almost breaking down as she allowed herself to think the worst. 'He's my whole world – you know that, Zach. What am I going to do if we never get Red Star back?'

CHAPTER ELEVEN

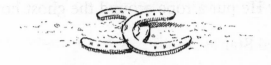

Keira's mom and dad called everyone they knew.

'We lost Keira's pony. A horse thief took him. If you see him, be sure to let us know.'

Then they called every sale barn and horse facility in the county. The message was the same – 'We're looking for a ten-year-old strawberry roan gelding. He was stolen from Black Pearl Ranch. Contact us if a tall, thin guy in a beaten-up white trailer tries to sell him to you.'

And of course they called the Sheriton sheriff. 'Sheriff Atwood? Allyson Lucas here. There's one horse thief still on the loose. He took Keira's pony along with the black gelding from Silver Spur. We need you to find out all you can from the two guys you caught early today.'

The sheriff said he would follow up the lead and told the Lucases to get some sleep. 'We'll find him,' he promised. 'We'll put out an alert. The traffic cops will pick him up before he's out of the county.'

By the time Allyson came off the phone it was almost midnight.

'The hospital X-rayed Josh and diagnosed concussion,' Jacob reminded everyone. 'No bones broken, hopefully no big deal. He'll be back home by Monday.'

'So everything there is good,' Allyson reassured Keira, Brooke and Zach. 'And the sheriff was right – we all need to sleep.'

Reluctantly Keira went upstairs. She felt like she was in a daze as she got undressed and brushed her teeth. *What am I going to do without you, Red Star?* she asked herself over and over. *How can I live without you?*

She went to bed and dreamed. First she dreamed about the ghost horse. He stood on a ridge in a world covered in snow – a black shape against a white hillside, only faintly visible amongst whirling snowflakes. He reared onto his hind legs, whinnied and galloped away. Then the dream switched to

Red Star. He was locked inside a dark trailer, his mane was matted, his eyes were dull.

'Red Star!' she whispered, but he didn't hear her. 'Red Star, it's me!' she repeated.

A man with a Stetson pulled low over his forehead led her pony out of the trailer into an arena. Red Star didn't want to go. He dug in his heels. But the guy jerked at the rope then whipped the knotted end against his side. Red Star tried to rear but the man hit him again and forced him into the arena. Another man called out numbers as shadowy figures bid to buy the strawberry roan.

Keira jerked awake. She sat up in bed, filled with dread. Everything was dark and her heart pounded. *It's a dream*, she told herself. *Only a dream.*

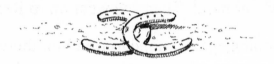

Dawn crept into the dark sky and Keira was already up and dressed. Black Pearl Mountains were flat and grey in the half-light. Down in the kitchen, Popcorn yawned, stretched and left his basket to come and rub against Keira's legs.

She sighed and picked him up. His fur felt warm and soft against her cheek. 'What am I going to do?' she whispered, feeling that her heart would break.

She pulled on her boots and went out to the barn, stepping through puddles left by the melted snow. One by one she stroked the horses in their warm stalls – Annie, Captain, Misty, Sonny. They lowered their heads, breathed over her and quietly nuzzled her hand. Then she went on to Red Star's stall, hoping against hope to find him there. But it was empty. Keira turned and walked blindly out of the barn.

Her mom found her gazing out across the flooded meadow.

'We will find him,' Allyson said firmly. She leaned on the fence and watched the sun warm up the mountains.

'Red Star was born the day I was born,' Keira sighed. 'We're like twins.'

'I know, honey. I know how hard this is.' They stood a while staring at the horizon. Then Allyson put her arm around Keira's shoulder and led her back to the house, where everyone was up and Jacob was cooking bacon on a sizzling hot stove.

'Here's the plan,' Keira's dad said. 'I drive to the hospital with Brooke. We meet Kevin and talk through exactly what happened to Josh. Then we check up on the patient.'

'Say hi to Josh from me and Keira,' Allyson told him. 'Tell him to get well quick.'

'What about us, Mom?' Keira wanted to know. 'We can't sit here doing nothing.'

'What else is there?' Zach asked. 'We can't ride out to search for Red Star – we already know that the guy would drive the trailer as far away from here as he can get.'

'We wait for the sheriff to call,' Allyson decided as Brooke and Jacob got ready for the hospital trip.

Brooke searched on a shelf and found a book on wild mustangs that she thought Josh might like. Jacob called his brother, Kevin, to arrange where they should meet.

'Try to find a job to do,' Keira's dad suggested. 'Clean some tack, rake the corral – maybe it'll keep your mind off the problem.'

Keira agreed. But she wouldn't go near Red Star's empty stall, she decided. She would just keep busy.

Even so, time dragged. Minutes felt like hours and hours like days. The corral was raked smooth, the bits and bridles hung shining from their hooks.

She stood on the tack room porch in a kind of daze when Zach called her and ran from the house with news. 'The sheriff called. We have a name!'

'What name?' She was so sad and far away in her thoughts that at first she couldn't tune into what Zach was saying.

'Of the third guy who stole the horses. It's Jason Osmond. The two in jail spilled the beans.'

Slowly Keira nodded. 'So what now?' she muttered.

'Wait – there's more.' Zach's face was flushed and he spoke so fast that his tongue tripped up over his words. 'The traffic cops found the trailer.'

She gasped and suddenly everything came back into focus. 'Where?' she asked. 'When? How's Red Star?'

'Hold it.' Zach grabbed her arm as she jumped down from the porch and began to run for the

house. 'The trailer broke down by Sharman Lake.'

'Where exactly? Come on – let's go!' Keira saw her mom stride out of the house and hold up her car keys, ready for action. Her heart soared. They'd found the trailer, they'd found the ponies. Red Star was safe!

'Wait,' Zach insisted. 'It was on the highway,

right on the county line. The cops investigated the trailer but it was empty.'

She stopped dead, her heart plummeted. There was a sick feeling in her stomach as she turned to look at Zach. 'Empty?' she echoed.

He nodded. 'They say Osmond unloaded Red Star and the ghost horse.'

'So where did he take them?' Keira whispered. She was down, up and down again on a roller-coaster. The dread came back and dipped her so far down, so fast she could hardly breathe.

'They reckon he could have led them on foot over the county line,' Zach explained. 'This guy is no fool. He took them into Norton County. Now we start over – a new search, new cops, the whole deal.'

CHAPTER TWELVE

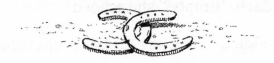

The Sunday morning traffic was light as Allyson, Zach and Keira rode the highway to Sharman Lake. Still, Allyson kept to the speed limits through the small towns, seeming to Keira to crawl past convenience stores and gas stations.

'Step on it, Mom!' she pleaded. At last they'd passed the county sign that took them into Norton County and in the distance up ahead she could see the glimmer of Sharman Lake nestling between two high peaks.

'I'm going as fast as the law lets me,' Allyson replied. She swung off the highway up a winding road, following a sign that said 'Sharman Lake, 2 miles'.

Now Keira and Zach had to hang on as the car took the hairpin bends and the road sloped steeply

down. 'Look out for the trailer,' Zach warned, and they kept their eyes peeled.

'There!' Keira saw it first – the same dust-covered trailer she'd seen Osmond drive off in, with its buckled fender and missing registration plate. The thief had abandoned it in the entrance to a driveway, under a wooden arch with a creaking sign which read 'Clinton's Sale Barn'.

Allyson braked and pulled up behind the trailer. Keira and Zach leaped out and ran to look inside.

'Empty,' Zach confirmed.

Keira climbed in and searched in every dark corner, just in case. Red Star had been here for sure – she picked up his lead rope, still with the lasso loop which Osmond had made attached. Then she found a chunk of his red and black saddle blanket caught on a bolt. She was taking it out to show her mom when a man's voice interrupted them.

'Don't mess with that trailer.'

Zach, Allyson and Keira looked down the rutted driveway to see what looked like the owner of the barn approaching. He was a heavy-set guy in a brown leather jacket and dusty Stetson, and no way did he look happy to see them.

'The sheriff and his deputy are out back, searching my barn,' he warned. 'That trailer contains evidence of a robbery.'

Keira's mom ironed out a frown and offered the man her hand. 'Allyson Lucas,' she said. 'We're the people who were robbed.'

'Jed Clinton,' he grunted without shaking Allyson's hand. 'I already told the cops I don't know anything about stolen horses.'

'But did you see the driver of the trailer?' Allyson asked.

'Tall and mean looking,' Keira chipped in. 'He stole my pony, Red Star.'

'Plus a black gelding from Silver Spur, out near High Peak,' Zach said.

'Osmond didn't try to offload them onto you?' Allyson checked.

Clinton shook his head. 'I already told the cops – I run a law-abiding operation.'

'OK, thanks. I'll talk to the sheriff,' Allyson decided. She stepped past Clinton and walked towards a shabby, red-painted barn where a police car was parked in the doorway. Keira and Zach followed close behind.

'I don't think he's telling the truth!' Keira muttered to Zach.

'Yeah – me neither. I reckon he's in this with Osmond.'

'I'm sure Red Star is around here somewhere.'

Keira looked right and left at meadows flattened by the recent snowfall, and at a yard beside the barn which was full of ancient, rusting vehicles. Beyond that was a row of outbuildings – probably hay and feed stores.

'We could go take a look,' Zach suggested.

'No, let's do this properly,' Allyson said. She stopped beside the police car and called into the barn. 'Is the sheriff there, please?'

A guy in uniform emerged. He was aged around forty, with thinning grey hair and a relaxed manner. 'That would be me. Who wants to know?'

Quickly, Allyson introduced herself and equally rapidly the sheriff of Norton County filled in the facts. 'I have a guy searching the property as we speak,' he assured her. 'Clinton has more than thirty horses in his stalls, plus half a dozen more in the outbuildings – all waiting to be sold off in the next sale.'

'And?' Allyson prompted.

'So far – nothing. No black geldings, no strawberry roans.'

'But that's definitely Osmond's trailer,' Allyson told him.

'Which has been there since late yesterday afternoon,' the sheriff pointed out. 'It's possible that Osmond switched the stolen horses into one of Clinton's trailers and drove off with them.'

'No.' Keira shook her head. She kept tight hold of the scrap of saddle blanket and spoke so that only Zach could hear. 'That's not right. Red Star is still here – I know it!'

'You want to take a look?' Zach whispered.

She nodded and they took their chance to slip away when Clinton strode angrily between the sheriff and her mom. 'I told you – you won't find any stolen horses in my barn,' he insisted, his face mottled, his voice a low growl. 'This is an honest outfit!'

Leaving the grown-ups to argue, Keira and Zach slipped down the side of the main barn and between the rusty trucks and tractors towards the neglected outbuildings.

'Let's look in here,' Keira hissed, opening a door and stepping inside.

'Whoa!' Zach covered his mouth and nose. 'This place stinks!'

Keira nodded and backed out. The shed was

stacked with rotting hay bales. The next one was no better – full of old farm tools, with parts of oily engines scattered about the dirt floor. They moved onto the shed furthest down the line. 'Better, huh?' Zach said as he opened the door.

Keira looked over his shoulders at a row of stalls. 'Yeah,' she muttered, 'this is more like it.' She entered quickly and went down the line, checking out a forlorn paint pony then two sorrels and an Appaloosa. 'Hey.' She greeted them softly as she went by. Then she came to two empty stalls and peered inside. There was trampled straw on the floor, a water bucket in each and an open door at the end of the row leading out onto a meadow overlooking Sharman Lake.

'Red Star!' Keira murmured. She was one

hundred per cent certain that this is where the thief had brought him. 'This time!' she promised. 'This time we won't let him get away!'

'Come on!' Zach was the first to react. He ran through the door into the marshy meadow, picked up a track and followed it.

Taking a deep breath, Keira followed. She saw the trail – deep prints in the mud – then looked ahead at the lake spreading before them, still covered in a thin layer of ice. She ran hard to catch up with Zach.

The mud sucked at their feet and slowed them down as they followed the trail right to the water's edge.

'Where did he go from here?' Zach wanted to know. It was as if Osmond had taken the two ponies into the lake and vanished.

But Keira spotted where the ice was broken. The trail led along the shoreline towards a bunch of aspens. She took it up again and before she'd taken ten more paces she spotted something among the trees. 'Red Star!' she yelled.

Panicked by her cry, two blue jays rose from the trees and flapped off across the lake. At the same time, a horse replied with a high whinny.

'Red Star!' Keira said again. He knew her voice. He was calling out to her. 'I'm coming!' she yelled.

She ran along the lake shore, crunching the crust of ice, slipping and sliding in her haste. Yes – now she could see them; Osmond riding her beloved pony, dragging the ghost horse along. The thief spurred Red Star on through the trees, the pony

resisted. They blundered sideways into a tree, stepped clumsily onto the ice.

'Stop!' Keira yelled, running and narrowing the gap.

Red Star whinnied again. He could definitely hear Keira. He turned his head to see her drawing near.

Osmond kicked, Red Star reared. He was crunching through thin ice, up on his hind legs, flinging his rider back in the saddle.

'Aaagh!' Osmond let out a cry. He lost the reins and groped for the saddle horn, missed it and was thrown clear.

Keira heard the crack of ice and a mighty splash as the thief landed in the lake. She watched him struggle, saw the icy waters swallow him. But she

didn't care – she ran towards Red Star and grabbed

his reins. She flung her arms around his neck, laid

her face against his neck and wept for joy.

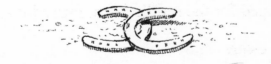

It had taken the sheriff and his deputy less than two

minutes to reach the lake and drag Osmond from

the freezing water. They'd heard the shout from

Keira, then Osmond's frightened yell, and they'd broken away from Allyson and Clinton to sprint to the rescue. They'd arrested the dripping, shivering thief and taken him and Clinton away in their car. Soon after that, Jacob and Brooke had driven over from the hospital in Elk Springs to pick up Red Star and the ghost horse.

'We called the Silver Spur and gave Marie Shawcross the good news,' Jacob had informed them. 'She can come and collect her gelding any time she likes.'

And now it was evening and the family was back home at Black Pearl Ranch. The ghost horse was safe in the barn with Annie and the others and Keira stood with Red Star at the gate to the meadow, looking out over their favourite view.

'Hey, Keira – you want me to lay new straw in his stall?' Zach called from the barn door.

She turned and nodded. She and Red Star didn't plan to move from their spot – not until the sinking sun had turned red and slipped down behind the mountains.

'How's it feel to be home?' Keira whispered into Red Star's ear.

He lowered his head and nuzzled her cheek. *Pretty good.*

'Great news!' Brooke called from the house

porch. 'Uncle Kevin called to say they let Josh out of the hospital early!'

'Cool!' Keira called back.

Everything was coming good. The sun was sinking, glowing gold and red on the black horizon.

'Time to eat!' Allyson called everyone for their supper.

Still Keira stood at the gate with her arm around Red Star's neck. He breathed in and out, in and out – unhurried, steady. There was no breeze, the whole world was silent.

Finally Jacob came to fetch Keira and Red Star. 'Take your pony into the barn then come into the house,' he told her gently.

'Soon,' she promised.

Her dad squeezed Keira's hand. 'Relax – he's safe now,' he whispered as he went back to the house.

So Keira walked her pony across the corral. As he followed her into his stall, she knew her dad was right. Red Star was back where he belonged.

Tonight she would dream again of the ghost horse in the snow, and this time the dream would have a happy ending. She would rescue the beautiful black gelding and take him home. Then, in a dream that would stay with her for a lifetime, she would ride Red Star off the trail, along a ridge with the sun on her face and wind in her hair. They would be happy and free.

Keira's home is **Black Pearl Ranch**, where she helps train ponies – and lives the dream …

Black Pearl Ponies

RED STAR

Red Star is the love of Keira's life and the best pony ever. But he's in danger: he's gone missing in the snowy mountains, home to bears and coyotes.

Has he escaped? Or has he been stolen? Either way, can Keira rescue her beloved pony in time?